KATIE'S TOO~BIG COAT

SIMON & SCHUSTER BOOKS FOR YOUNG READERS
Published By Simon & Schuster
New York   London   Toronto   Sydney   Tokyo   Singapore

KATIE'S TOO~BIG COAT

By Jane Stephens · Illustrated by Nancy Poydar

SIMON & SCHUSTER BOOKS FOR YOUNG READERS
Simon & Schuster Building, Rockefeller Center
1230 Avenue of the Americas, New York, New York 10020.
Text copyright © 1993 by Jane Stephens.
Illustrations copyright © 1993 by Nancy Poydar.
SIMON & SCHUSTER BOOKS FOR YOUNG READERS
is a trademark of Simon & Schuster.
Designed by Vicki Kalajian.
The text of this book is set in 16 point ITC Garamond Light.
The illustrations were done in watercolors with colored pencils.

Manufactured in the United States of America

10 9 8 7 6 5 4 3 2 1
Library of Congress Cataloging-in-Publication Data
Stephens, Jane. Katie's too-big coat / by Jane Stephens ;
illustrated by Nancy Poydar.
Summary: Katie dislikes her too-large coat, until the day
the wind puffs it up like a balloon and blows
her into the sky for an exciting adventure.
[1. Coats—Fiction.   2. Winds—Fiction.]   I. Poydar, Nancy, ill.
II. Title.   PZ7.M827242Kat 1993   [E]—dc20 CIP 91-42805
ISBN 0-671-77774-2

For their help in all
the little inspirations—
James, Robert, Aaron, Kelly,
Alex, and Boo
—JS

To Anna E. Poydar
and the memory of Henry F. Poydar
—NP

The day Aunt Mary came to visit, she gave
Katie a present. It was a coat, and it was too big.
  "It's lovely," said Katie's mom.
  "I like it, too," Katie agreed. "But it's too big."
  "Nonsense," her aunt said. "It gives you room
to grow."

Well, Katie thought, Mom and Aunt Mary might
like it, but IT WAS TOO BIG!

The next day, Katie had to wear her too-big coat to school.

It was very windy. As soon as Katie stepped outside her house, the wind blew up the sleeves of her too-big coat, and the wind blew down the collar. Before too long, Katie's coat was all puffed up like a balloon!

Suddenly, a great big gust of
wind rushed up the sleeves
and down the collar, and away
she flew—up and up and up!

"Help!" she cried to her mom.

But she blew away too fast
for her mom to catch her.

"Help!" she called to the bus
driver in the big yellow school
bus.

But the bus driver missed
her, too.

Katie blew down the street. "Help!" she cried to the fire fighters in the firehouse.

But their ladders were too short to reach her.

"Help!" she shouted to the crane operator on top of the building.

But the crane could not swing around fast enough to help her.

Katie blew across the football field. "Help!"
she yelled to the football players on the
fifty-yard line.

But she soared too high for them to tackle her.

Katie blew across the park. "Help!" she called
to the butterfly collector with his great big net.
But his net was not big enough for Katie's
too-big coat and away she blew.

"Help!" she cried to the news reporters in the helicopter who were taking pictures for the six o'clock news.

But the wind from the helicopter made Katie somersault through the air, and the reporters had to fly away.

Katie blew over the zoo. "Help!" she called
to the giraffe with his tall, thin neck.
    But his neck was not tall enough to reach
Katie.
    "Help!" she cried to the elephants with their
long, long trunks.

But their trunks were full of water, and they just got Katie all wet.

"Help!" Katie cried again.

But the monkeys and the alligators and the bears could only watch in amazement as Katie blew away.

"Help!" Katie whispered to a flock of birds.
But the wind swept Katie behind a puffy white
cloud, and the birds could not find her.

Katie blew down Main Street, right into the middle of a big parade.

"Look, there's a girl in that balloon!" cried a boy in the crowd as Katie blew by, all mixed up with the balloons and the floats.

"Help!" she shouted to the crowd.

But the crowd thought she was part of the parade and cheered her on.

The wind blew Katie to the fair,
where a huge Ferris wheel turned
round and round.

Katie held out her hand and
stretched, stretched, stretched to
reach the Ferris wheel.

She got it!

Katie went over the top of the wheel and all
the way down.

Whoosh! went all the air out of her coat as her
feet touched the ground.

"I almost blew all the way around the world!"
Katie cried, glad to be out of the sky.

"Katie," said her mom. "I think we'll get you a smaller coat."

Katie shook her head, thinking of all the fun she had had today. "Oh no, Mom. I like this one, it's just big enough to grow in."